30 DAYS TO SAVE YOUR MARRIAGE

The Handbook that may help save your marriage.

By: Dr. Willard L. Smith and Dr. Karen Hollie-Smith

Table of Content

Introduction

If you are reading this handbook you are reading it because you either like the title, or you are in a troubled marriage, or you are being proactive so that you do not face those times when you have to decide to stay or leave.

The book is intended for marriages as God has ordained and though we recognize every person's right, according to the world, to marry as they wish, we hold to marriages as defined by one man and one woman. We respect the opinions of others and ask that others do the same for us. Thank you for understanding.

To be fair and transparent, my wife and I have both experienced moments when that question of whether to leave or stay troubled our thoughts, not toward each other, but in relationships before our meeting. Sometimes people simply make bad decisions as it relates to who they will marry. Other times, it is not the decision that drives you apart, but the mindset, habits, or even lack of attention needed in the marriage. Some marriages simply cannot work, but some marriages can work with a little adjustment.

It is said that one of the biggest issues in marriages is for each person to resist wanting things their way. In a marriage, there is always some form of compromise and without compromise, the challenge of staying together becomes more difficult as the years go by.

My wife is a Clinical Psychotherapist and I cannot tell you how many stories she has about couples who struggle in their marriage. She gives the best advice and counsel that you can imagine, but without the couple putting a plan of action in place, even her excellent counsel falls short of saving the marriage. I am sure that those who took her advice and put it to work, no matter how difficult it may have been to come to that place, at the least saw improvement in their relationship, if not a complete turnaround in their marriage.

This handbook is a result of conversations that my wife and I have had and our efforts to help other couples by sharing practical information that, if used, will help your marriage or even turn things around for you.

It is our deepest prayer that if you are trying to move forward together, this handbook gives you keys that will help.

All the best to you,

Dr. Will and Dr. Karen

Our Prayer for you and your marriage

Father, in the name of Jesus, we are thankful to you that you saw that it was not good for a man to be alone, so you gave him a help meet. We thank you that the two become one when you join them together and that marriage was your idea.

Father, _____ and _____ entered into marriage and have come to a challenging place, but your word has promised us that we can come to you in prayer and you will grant us an answer.

Father, we ask that you look upon the two of them and place Angels all around them so that they can be guided in the right direction for their marriage. Father, cause them to search their hearts to determine their motive and desires for their marriage and to come to a place of decision as to whether it is your will for them to move forward and as to if they each desire to walk in that will. Father, place people around them that will encourage their union and remove all outside forces and people that may cause division. Give them both the presence of mind to focus on your word and your instructions to each as husband and wife. Grant revelations of your word to them so that they grow stronger in their faith. Give them a quiet spirit so that they do not speak the wrong word in moments of bitterness or anger. Speak to their minds and break through their hearts so that their affection and love will rekindle and so that they have the mind to put forth the effort to do kind gestures to each other.

Father, any negative thoughts that they may have against each other, we put under the blood of Jesus and we speak faith-filled words into their hearing so that the words and thoughts of their husband or wife line up with your thoughts concerning each.

Father, thank you for doing in the spirit what cannot be done naturally for them. Father, give them each the heart and mind of forgiveness toward each other. Lord, let their love, romance, unity, and successes as a couple cause them to see your power at work in them. Lastly, Lord, use them to help other couples understand the power of staying together. In Jesus' name, Amen!

How to use this handbook

This handbook is not designed to be the "cure-all, end-all," instead it is designed to provide you with 30 days of activity that each of you should do to help foster growth and unity in your marriage. We realize that even though the daily tasks are simple, they may be difficult at first because if your marriage is troubled, there is a chance that you will struggle to want to do anything at all with the other person. That is normal because when you are challenged in a relationship, the reality is that most people spend more time thinking of ways to not be bothered with the other person than they do thinking about how to bring it back together and move forward healthily.

We encourage you to spend time in prayer daily, not for your wife or husband, but for yourself. Ask God to help you deal with your attitude and any negative thoughts toward your partner. As David, in the scripture said, " Create in me a clean heart O' God and renew the right spirit in me." (Psalm 51:10 King James Version -Create in me a clean heart. The condition of your heart will be important in moving forward.

To get the most out of this handbook, simply perform the daily activities with all of your heart and keep in mind, you are doing this so that you can see a more unified marriage at the end of the 30 days. You must want this 30-day period to work for you. You must joyfully put all of your energy into doing the task from your heart with the thought that you are being a blessing to the other person.

My wife and I wish you the best and we believe that the next 30 days will prove to be an answer to your prayers for your marriage. We are praying for you and we know that you are praying for your mate.

Day 1

Take time to write a prayer to God for your partner

Example: " God help us to………….. "

" God, our marriage is in trouble and we need you to……….."

The key is to write down the things that you want God to do for your marriage. You can do this together. Try to stay positive in your request and try not to be offended if your mate says something that you do not agree with. Remember that you likely came to this place of the challenge because one or the other did not understand the concern of the other.

-

_____

_____

_____

_____

_____

_____

_____

_____

Day 2

Locate photos of the times that you were happy and make a scrapbook together.

You can glue the photos to the blank pages that follow.

Day 3

Say 7 positive things to each other throughout the day. Please make sure that they are sincere.

Take the time to share a positive word with your mate throughout this day. Don't try to say all 7 of them at once. The idea is to spread them throughout the day. Try to say them in person, but if you are not near, you can text, call, email, or any other creative way that you may come up with. Some people may have a hard time thinking of 7 things to say, so here is a sample list:

" You are so lovely"

" I love the way you……"

" I am thankful for you because….."

" No one else has ever……."

" You do a wonderful job at……."

Day 4

Write 5 things that your mate has done for you.

This could be a kind gesture, a feeling, or even a task that you appreciated or benefited from.

1._____

2._____

3._____

4._____

5. _____

Day 5

Write about the best day that you have had with your mate

Tell the story of the event. Tell the story of what happened to make you feel it was the best day

together.

_____

_____

_____

_____

_____

_____

_____

_____

_____

_____

_____

_____

_____

_____

Day 6

Take a walk together in the park or your neighborhood. Pre-record a message on your telephone that speaks of things that worked in the marriage. During your walk, each person will play the pre-recorded message for the other person to hear. You can hold hands or you don't have to. The idea is to be together and to allow the walk to be a time to reflect on positive things that promote your marriage. Write your outcome below. How do you feel now? What were some of your positive thoughts as you were walking?

_____

_____

_____

_____

_____

_____

_____

_____

_____

_____

_____

Day 7

Listen to your favorite love song together

The idea behind this exercise is for the two of you to sit together and listen to your favorite love song. It could be the love song of his choice or the love song of your choice or even a song that you both choose. As you simply sit and listen, try to focus on the words to the song and try to see if there are words in the song that describe how you feel about the person.

What did you feel after this exercise?

_____

_____

_____

_____

_____

_____

_____

_____

_____

_____

_____

Day 8

Go have a scoop of ice cream together

The idea behind this exercise is to simply have a pleasurable moment together. Even if you don't eat ice cream, have a fun snack together.

What are your thoughts now that you have completed this task?

_____

_____

_____

_____

_____

_____

_____

_____

_____

_____

_____

_____

_____

_____

Day 9

Take a trip to the local store together to shop for greeting cards for each other. The husband should select one for his wife and the wife should select one for her husband. Once you have purchased the card, go home and write something on the card. Set aside time to exchange them and each person should read the card to the other person.

How do you feel now that you have exchanged cards?

_____

_____

_____

_____

_____

_____

_____

_____

_____

_____

_____

_____

_____

Day 10

Prepare a small breakfast for each other and serve each other in bed, Enjoy breakfast as you carry on a conversation.

The idea behind this exercise is to do something for your mate that allows you to serve them and then enjoy their company.

How do you feel now that you have served each other?

_____

_____

_____

_____

_____

_____

_____

_____

_____

_____

_____

_____

Day 11

The husband should plan an activity. Plan an activity that the two of you can do together. The wife does not have to like the activity, simply carry it out with him.

The idea behind this exercise is for the two of you to come together and enjoy the activity together. Some ideas are:

- In-house picnic

- Watch a television show together and discuss it.

- Play a board game

- Do a crossword puzzle together

- Other

Write something about the activity and how you felt after you finished it.

-

_____

_____

_____

_____

_____

_____

_____

_____

Day 12

The wife should plan an activity. Plan an activity that the two of you can do together. The husband does not have to like the activity, simply carry it out with her.

The idea behind this exercise is for the two of you to come together and enjoy the activity together.

How do you feel now that you have completed the activity?

_____

_____

_____

_____

_____

_____

_____

_____

_____

_____

_____

_____

_____

Day 13

Have a cup of coffee, your favorite beverage, or tea, and talk about the day that you met. Discuss things like:

- What attracted you to him/her?

- Were you afraid to approach him/her?

How do you feel now that you have discussed these questions?

_____

_____

_____

_____

_____

_____

_____

_____

_____

_____

_____

_____

_____

Day 14

Do kind deeds throughout the day for each other. Ideas may include:

- Iron each other's clothes

- Rub each other's feet

- Offer to read a story to your mate

- Wash the clothes

- Other

How do you feel now that you have spent your day serving your mate?

_____

_____

_____

_____

_____

_____

_____

_____

_____

_____

_____

Day 15

Go on an outing together. Take a moment to simply go for a ride, go see a movie, or even go get a donut together. The idea is to get out of the house to do something together.

How do you feel now that you have finished this exercise?

_____

_____

_____

_____

_____

_____

_____

_____

_____

_____

_____

_____

Day 16

Re-enact your first date. Whatever you did on your first date do it again exactly like you did it then or at least come close to doing it the way you did it.

The idea behind this exercise is to bring the two of you together and to spark the love that you shared from the beginning of your relationship.

How did you feel after this exercise?

_____

_____

_____

_____

_____

_____

_____

_____

_____

_____

_____

_____

_____

Day 17

Spend $20.00 on a simple gift and exchange it with your mate. Keep in mind, it is not the gift that is most important but the act of the two of you exchanging the gifts. If you want to add to this exercise, simply share your reason behind selecting that gift.

_____

_____

_____

_____

_____

_____

_____

_____

_____

_____

_____

_____

Day 18

Each one of you writes a letter to the other entitled, " What I think a good marriage looks like."

Once the letter is written, select a time to exchange letters and if you desire, read the letter to

each other. Do not dispute the other person's ideas, simply try to understand their view and make

adjustments as you are so led. The letter is not a reflection of the challenges that your marriage

may be facing. You are simply defining your view of a successful marriage.

What do you think about your mate's letter?

_____

_____

_____

_____

_____

_____

_____

_____

_____

_____

_____

_____

Day 19

Act out a famous couple that you admire and have your partner guess who it is.

_____

_____

_____

_____

_____

_____

_____

_____

_____

_____

_____

_____

_____

Day 20

Ask her what she likes to do and do it with her. The idea is for you to do something with her that she enjoys whether you enjoy it or not. Show her that you have an interest in what she enjoys.

_____

_____

_____

_____

_____

_____

_____

_____

_____

_____

_____

_____

_____

Day 21

Do something that he likes to do. Show him that you can embrace things that he likes.

How do you feel after you did what he likes?

_____

_____

_____

_____

_____

_____

_____

_____

_____

_____

_____

_____

_____

Day 22

Find an area of your home to clean together. This could be the garage, the living room, a closet, the backyard, the front yard, or, wherever you choose. The idea is to work together. It may be a good idea to decide on the area first and discuss how you expect it to look after you finish. Make it fun, take photos before and after.

How do you feel after finishing this project?

_____

_____

_____

_____

_____

_____

_____

_____

_____

_____

_____

_____

Day 23

Go to your local craft store together and each person selects a craft that they enjoy or want to learn. Work on the craft together. The idea is to work together for the completion of one or both.

How do you feel now that you have put the craft together?

_____

_____

_____

_____

_____

_____

_____

_____

_____

_____

_____

_____

Day 24

Take the time today to take a photo together. Try to dress alike. It does not matter whether you use your telephone or go to a professional studio. Take photos with several poses. You can smile, act silly, look serious, or do whatever you like. You can even change outfits. The idea here is to take pictures for future memories.

If possible, post photos below:

Day 25

Choose a different dish to cook that you have not cooked before and do it together. It can be a Mexican dish, an Indian dish, or whatever you like. This will require you to work together. Once you have finished preparing it, sit down and enjoy it together. It may be fun to divide up who cooks what.

How was the experience of cooking together?

_____

_____

_____

_____

_____

_____

_____

_____

_____

_____

_____

_____

Day 26

Do a humanitarian project together. Take the time to be a blessing to someone in need. Do this together.

Examples of projects that you can do:

- Prepare meals for the homeless and deliver them to either a shelter or individuals.

- Collect clothes for women who are living in shelters and deliver them to them.

- Volunteer together at your local boy's club, girls club, or other community-based organizations.

What was your project?_____

How do you feel now that you have completed this task?

_____

_____

_____

_____

_____

_____

_____

Day 27

Spend 30 minutes together praying, reading the bible, meditating, or even watching your favorite television channel together. When you finish, discuss what you learned with your mate.

How did the exercise help your marriage?

_____

_____

_____

_____

_____

_____

_____

_____

_____

_____

_____

_____

_____

Day 28

Find a childhood toy that you once enjoyed, and share it with your mate. Explain to them why it was your favorite toy. If it was something that you can both play with together, try playing together. You will be amazed at the fun you will have together. Examples of childhood toys (depending on your age):

- Marbles
- Checkers
- Barbie doll house
- Easy-bake oven
- Jack
- Other

How did you feel after you played together?

_____

_____

_____

_____

_____

_____

_____

_____

Day 29

Purchase two flower pots with flowers. The man should give his plant, his name and the woman should give her plant her name. Exchange plants so that the woman has the plant with her husband's name and the man has the plant with his wife's name on it. The idea is for each person to water and care for the plant daily as a reminder to them that they should water and care for each other daily. The goal is to keep the plant alive. If the plant dies, the person must go purchase another one and repeat the process.

How did the exercise help you?

_____

_____

_____

_____

_____

_____

_____

_____

_____

_____

_____

Day 30

Make a time capsule together. A time capsule is a container filled with historical things that the two of you can discover in a future period. You can choose to open it in two years or so, or you can give it to your children for future viewing.

- Movie tickets

- Photos

- Non-perishable snacks

- Books

- Vision Board

Final Assignment

Congratulations!

If you have made it to this page, you have likely completed all 30-day assignments and prayerfully, you have seen change or improvements in your marriage. You should have also taken the time to decide to continue to fight for your marriage, which means there is more work to be done.

The last part of this assignment is to create a plan of action with your mate. The plan of action is simply written goals and the steps that you will take to keep your marriage together.

The template below is just one that is easy to use. You can find or design your own based on your needs in the marriage. Feel free to use this one if you like

In the space below write the goals that you have for each area and initial the line. Discuss this plan monthly to track how you are doing in a given area. Since each couple has unique circumstances, you may write those things that are important to you both in the given area.

MARRIAGE PLAN OF ACTION

FOR

AND

_____ _____

What will we do to improve our communication?

_____ How often?_____ Initial_____ _____

Are there financial concerns?_____ What is our plan to change that circumstance?

_____

_____

_____Initial_____ _____

Do we spend enough time together?_____ What can we do to improve in this area?

_____

_____

_____Intial_____ _____

Other goals (Remember to initial them)

_____

_____

_____

_____

_____

This a helpful article for you

Unhappy in the marriage

16 signs you're in an unhappy marriage:
1.

There's constant criticism

Constant criticism is an indication that feelings of love and warmth for each other are being replaced by judgment. If you're constantly criticizing each other, that's not a good sign, according to the licensed therapist and co-founder of Viva Wellness Jor-El Caraballo, LMHC. "Criticism or name-calling is a huge boundary violation," adds licensed marriage and family therapist Shane Birkel, LMFT.
.

2.

Your relationship has become sexless

Another sign of an unhappy marriage is virtually nonexistent sex life. Or, when you do have sex on rare occasions, it's not great. Of course, not having sex all the time isn't necessarily a bad thing, and some couples don't mind a sexless relationship. It's not so much about how often married couples have sex; rather, it's about whether you enjoy sex with your spouse and feel good about your shared sex life.
3.

You struggle to spend time together

Being around each other may feel like a chore, or extremely forced. Without the sense of intimacy that was once there, you may feel like you have nothing to say—and also don't care what they have to say.
4.

You stop sharing wins

When something exciting happens, who's the first one you call? If it was once your spouse and now it's a friend or family member, that's a sign your marriage has taken a hit. Birkel notes that in unhappy marriages, there isn't much motivation to connect or share anything.
5.

You're both defensive

Caraballo and Birkel both note that constant defensiveness is a sure sign that the two of you aren't communicating well, going hand in hand with constant criticism. Simple statements or questions can also be met with backlash. For example, when one partner reminds the other to do a chore, they may get defensive and say something along the lines of, "I already said I was going to do it—don't guilt-trip me."

6.

You avoid each other, as much as you can

Birkel says that generally avoiding each other is also an obvious sign that things aren't going well. You'll likely make separate plans and have no motivation to spend time together—all of which point to an unhappy marriage.
7.

You daydream about leaving

Fantasies of leaving or being single may start to pop up in your mind. You're becoming aware of the issues facing your marriage and how the marriage makes you feel, and it's inevitably causing you to think of other possibilities.
8.

There's an anxious versus avoidant attachment dynamic

Something Birkel has frequently noticed is a clash of attachment styles: "There's a spectrum of people who are pursuers," he explains, "who is kind of boundary-less and get their self-esteem from how the other person feels about them. And then there are withdrawers—conflict avoiders that don't want to talk about issues." In these scenarios, there's often a cycle of one pursuing and the other withdrawing, only to cause more subsequent pursuing and withdrawing.
9.

You feel more yourself when separate

When you first get together with your spouse, you're supposed to feel like they bring out the best in you, and that you like who you are around them. In an unhappy marriage, you'll feel more yourself when they're not around and may even dislike who you are around them.
10.

You stop arguing

Not arguing anymore roughly translates to the two of you not being willing to work through things anymore. Arguing isn't great, obviously, but at least it means you're still fighting for something. "Losing motivation to work through things with each other is a really bad sign."
11.

You're in denial about negative patterns

Whether you've been together for decades or you're just not keen on the idea of divorce, accepting you're in an unhappy marriage can be very difficult. This can result in denial, or an "inability to recognize negative patterns," Birkel says, adding, "if you don't recognize it, it's going to be very difficult to improve on your relationship."
12.

There's no understanding or compassion

Things like blame, judgment, and shaming will often take the front stage in an unhappy marriage, Birkel says, leaving little to no room for understanding or compassion. When something goes wrong or isn't working, no one's willing to give the other the benefit of the doubt, a supportive gesture, or even just a loving tone of voice.

13.

Body language changes
We can tell a lot from body language, and it's usually not too hard to read when you know what to look for. Very basically, you and your spouse may always angle yourselves away from each other, even when speaking. You may cross your arms or put your hands on your hips a lot, in a dominating or defensive manner.
14.

It feels physically wrong being together
Being in each other's presence is no longer warm and joyful and instead likely feels cold, awkward, and uncomfortable. This may show up in certain body language, such as the examples mentioned above, but it can also simply be an overwhelming feeling that you don't want to be physically near each other. A. marriage without intimacy may struggle to survive.
15.

You feel contempt toward each other
Along with defensiveness and criticism, contempt is one of the "Four Horsemen" of relationships described by The Gottman Institute, one of the leaders in relationship research, Caraballo explains. Contempt is a kind of extreme disdain for another person, akin to hatred and disgust. It's a lingering emotion, and it will make most encounters with your spouse unpleasant.
16.

You stonewall each other

The fourth and final "horseman," Caraballo says, is stonewalling. It essentially involves someone shutting down, particularly during the conflict. They might walk away or simply surrender to make the conflict go away and be left alone. Birkel adds that stonewalling shows an unwillingness to improve your relations

Contact Information

Dr. Willard L. Smith & Dr. Karen Hollie-Smith

Email: theofficialpowercoupleinc1@gmail.com

Life Publishing Inc

www.lifepublishinginc.com

Atlanta, Ga

Made in the USA
Las Vegas, NV
10 November 2024

11535745R00031